The Lady Blue's *Story*

Movie Geek

THE LADY BLUE'S STORY

WRITTEN BY: MOVIE GEEK

Copyright © 2013 by Movie Geek

THE LADY BLUE'S STORY

THE PAPERBACK EDITION

WRITTEN BY: MOVIE GEEK

Copyright © 2013 by Movie Geek

Book Written by: Movie Geek

Photos by: Dreamstime @ www.dreamstime.com

Book formatted, designed and published by: Shamonj Gifts LLC

Website: www.shamonjgifts.com

FB Fanpage: www.facebook.com/shamonjgifts

Email: shamonjgifts@gmail.com

Shamonj Gifts LLC's mission is to make a difference in nations of people lives through words, pictures, multimedia, and deeds. We are a publishing company that publishes books and magazines and provides marketing, branding, and graphic design services.

DEDICATIONS & ACKNOWLEDGEMENTS

This book is dedicated to the greatest singer in the world Whitney Houston, all her fans and everyone who enjoyed the movie called the Bodyguard. God Bless the Houston Family and we miss you Whitney Houston (Rest In Peace).

This book is also dedicated to my family, my friends, and all the people who have been supportive of everything that I have been working towards. This book is also dedicated to every person who love pop and R & B music. Last but not least, this book is also dedicated to all of you who purchased it.

WHY YOU SHOULD READ THIS BOOK

A long time ago, I was head over-heels for and in love with a great man of God. Of course, I would never mention his name. He and I used to talk on the phone years ago. We used to tell stories together. I started a sentence to the story, and he finished it. Then time went by, and he told me that he wanted to tell me a story. So I told him hold on let me get my pen and paper. He said, "No don't write this down! Just close your eyes and listen!" So I closed my eyes, and he began to tell me the story. As I closed my eyes, I could picture everything he was saying. After the story was over, I can remember how tears of sorrow ran down my cheeks. So that story stuck with me for many years. A few years later after that night, I began to remember that story and started writing it down. Now I could never write it the way he told it to me. However, I have my own talent and wrote down as much as I could remember and even added my own parts to it.

Why you should read this book? This book is a very touching story filled with love, action, drama, with different twists and turns. This book in a sense kind of reminds me a bit of the Body Guard. If you were a fan of the movie the Body Guard, then you would love this book. This book isn't a copycat of the Bodyguard, but it has some components from the Bodyguard such as a Caucasian man trying to protect a beautiful successful African American singer from danger. Whitney Houston is the main character of the Bodyguard, and she was the singer in the movie. The main characters in this book are an African American beautiful successful and popular R & B and Pop singer and a Caucasian male. The Caucasian male is trying to protect the singer from danger. I also rewrote this book as a contribution to remember Whitney Houston. If you're a Whitney Houston fan, I strongly believe that you're going to love the Lady Blue's Story. Thank you very much for purchasing this book. Sit back, relax, and enjoy the story. Happy reading! ☺

Thank you once again for purchasing this book. As a free gift from Movie Geek to you, I want you all to check out my site where you will be able to watch movies, TV shows, Documentaries, and much more for free. Also, you will get paid to watch it, refer others to the website, and you'll get paid when they watch movies too. If you love movies just as much as I do, this will be a great thing for you. Here is the link for you to sign up, http://giantcinema.com/spud/Shamonj

TABLE OF CONTENTS

CHAPTER 1

It was a dark stormy night; the crowd was lined up outside of Joe's Music Club. Everyone was shoving each other to the left and to the right while trying to enter the building. The fans were excited about hearing the beautiful musical talent. Her name was Lyric Blue Perkins. She was famous and known as the most talented multi-genre singer. She was an R & B and pop singer who had the most unique and talented voice that eyes ever seen and ears ever heard. A few hours later, the Bouncer opened the door, checked the Ids and allowed people to come through the door.

On this dark rainy night, a tall, gorgeous, Caucasian man with silky dark hair, green eyes, dimples in his cheeks and a six-pack walked into Joe's Music Club. He was dressed in a black suit, with a stylish tie, with matching black gators and a black trench coat on. The man who walked into Joe's Music Club walked into the club in a cool, calm and collected way with confidence. He had a demeanor about him that was inviting particularly for women. Women in the club were throwing themselves at him, but he turned them all away.

The fans were sitting at the bar drinking on their alcohol anticipating the performance of the beautiful Lady Blues.

"I'm looking for this woman," Demetrius said.

Demetrius pulled out a picture of the woman he was looking for, but all the men in the club were too busy drinking their alcohol and completely ignored Demetrius. Next he saw the club owner locking up his office.

"Excuse me sir," Demetrius said.

"May I help you?" Joe said.

"Do you know a woman named Lyric Perkins?" Demetrius said.

"I don't know any woman by that name!" Joe said.

Demetrius put the picture into the man's face.

"I know that you know this woman. Don't play dumb with me!" Demetrius said.

"Look man, I don't know whom you are, but you betta get out of my face!" Joe said.

The club owner Joe balled up his fist and tried to punch Demetrius, but he missed. Demetrius retaliated. He balled up his fist and punched Joe in the face. Then he shoved him to the wall and grabbed him by the collar.

"Don't you ever in your life try to put your hands on me! Dude, I'm only going to say this once again. I know that you know this woman now where is she! Now you better tell me or things could get ugly!" Demetrius said.

"If you don't take your hands off of me I will put you out of my club!" Joe said.

Finally a short, fat, dark skinned man came onto the stage.

"Greetings ladies and gentlemen; I want to thank you all for coming out tonight. The Lady Blue is in the house tonight. I want you all to put your hands together for the Lady Blue," Jeff said.

A beautiful woman walked on the stage. The audience started to cheer. All of a sudden the woman picked up the microphone.

"This song I am about to sing is dedicated to you if you've ever had a first time being in love," Lyric said.

Then the beautiful woman began to sing the song. She sang the song entitled "The First Time Ever I Saw Your Face." Then Demetrius turned around and saw the woman he was looking for singing on the stage. Next he let the man go and Joe left and went into his office. Then she started singing other songs. The crowed cheered loudly especially after she hit the high notes and held them. She also sang two other songs. She sang the song called "Seduces Me." Then she sang the song "All By Myself." After she finished singing the songs she bowed her head and the crowd stood and cheered loudly. They applauded and began to yell out her nicknames.

"Jazzy, Lady Blue, Jazzy, Lady Blue, Jazzy, Lady Blue, Jazzy, Lady Blue, Jazzy," the crowd yelled.

"Thank you," Lyric said softly and politely.

Then Lyric took a bow and left the stage. As Lyric was walking to her dressing room she stopped and heard two women and they talking mention her name.

"You know I sing a lot better than Jazzy," Katelyn said.

"Well you know how the crowed goes wild when Jazzy run to that stage," Sally replied.

"Well, I am tired of it. I am sick of being a back up singer here at this club. I think that they should make me head singer at this club. I would do a better job than Jazzy," Katelyn said.

"Well, Katelyn honey. Now you know that Jazzy is the moneymaker around here. She is the reason this club gets paid besides the alcohol. Let's say consequently something was to happen to her and she stopped singing. This club wouldn't make any money. People wouldn't have a reason to come here," Sally replied.

"Well, I don't like Jazzy, Lyric or whatever her name is. It's like she has turned this into her own personal club and Joe don't say a thing about it," Katelyn said with an attitude.

"Well you know something; we get paid every week and don't do anything. I am cool with that. I don't have to be a star or anything," Sally said.

After hearing all the negative things that the two women were saying about her, Lyric walked into her dressing room. Then she grabbed a few bottles of Whisky, Everclear and some Vodka and started drinking them.

Demetrius went into the restroom and stayed there. Joe's son Jeff returned to the stage.

"Did you all enjoy yourselves?" Jeff asked.

The crowd began to shout a thunderous scream and applauded.

"Ok, Crowd time to go. You don't have to go home but you have to get out of here," Jeff said.

A few hours later, people left Joe's club. Joe's workers cleaned the place up. Jeff counted the money. Then Joe wrote all the workers checks and put them into each mailbox. Lyric sat in her room for a while.

Once the coast seemed to be clear, Demetrius left the restroom and headed to Lyric's room. Her huge bodyguard saw him approaching the room so he stopped Demetrius in his tracks.

"Yo little man, you can't go in there," Bull Dog yelled at Demetrius while he was blocking the door to Lyric's dressing room.

"I need to speak to Lyric," Demetrius said,

"Fool you better get out of here! I said that you can't go back there!" Bull Dog said as he pushed Demetrius roughly.

"Look, I don't have time to play with you Biggie Smalls. I don't care what you said! You better move out of my way!" Demetrius said.

Demetrius trying to be a tough guy put all his strength into trying to move Bull Dog (Lyric's Big Bodyguard). Then Bull Dog slammed Demetrius and threw him across the room and he hit the wall and fell on the floor. Lyric heard noises so she ran outside the room.

"What is going on out here?" She yelled.

"This fool keeps trying to come into your room," Bull Dog said.

"Both of you need to stop all that fighting and arguing," She yelled.

"Lyric, I have something important to talk to you about. Please listen to me," Demetrius said.

"Yo Lyric, do you want to talk to this loser? Because if you don't I can pick him up and throw him out of the club," Bull Dog said.

"Let him in, I want to see what he want," She said.

Demetrius stuck his tongue out at Bull Dog and mumbled under his breath.

"Now what fool! Don't make me kick your butt!" Demetrius said.

"What did you say fool?" Bull Dog said.

"Come in!" Lyric said.

Demetrius walked into the room and shut the door.

"You wanted to see me right, you have 5 minutes to talk," Lyric said.

"Yes, Lyric I have something very important to talk to you about," Demetrius said.

Suddenly, Lyric raised her hand and smacked Demetrius on the face.

"Ouch woman, what did you do that for?" He yelled out of anger.

"I would suggest that you lower your voice or Bull Dog will come in here first of all," Lyric said.

"Woman, why did you smack me?" He asked.

"How could you do this to me? Why did you come back into my life? What do you want from me Demetrius Woods?" Lyric said.

"Lyric, what is wrong with you? You are not the same Lyric that I was once around as a child. This is not the life for you. There is more to life than being around these ignorant people at the bar. Your mom raised you better than that," Demetrius said.

"Damn you. Who are you to tell me what to do with my life? This is my life. I've got lots of money in the bank. They pay me well here. I'm doing damn good! My family comes to see me every night. You can't come back into my life and mess things up for me," Lyric said.

Demetrius' face turned red and he became frustrated.

"These people are not your family. They are a bunch of drunks who don't care about you," Demetrius said.

"A bunch of drunks who pay to hear me sing night after night," She said.

"Lyric, these people are not your family. They are only a bunch of drunks. They don't care about you. I am your family. Your mother is your family. She need you," Demetrius said.

"She don't need me. I have not heard from her in years. I am doing fine without her and I am pretty sure she is doing fine without me! Also you're not my damn family," Lyric said.

Lyric reached for a bottle of Hennessey and started to drink out the bottle.

"Lyric, you don't drink," Demetrius said.

"You don't know what I do!" Lyric said.

Demetrius saw that Lyric was drinking too much so he snatched the bottle from her hand.

"What the hell is you doing Demetrius?" Lyric said.

"You don't need to be drinking that liquor like that," Demetrius said.

"I'm a grown ass woman and I do what the hell I want to do!" Lyric yelled.

"Lyric, what has happened to you? You are not the same girl I have known for many years," Demetrius said.

"I am not that same girl that you knew back in Georgia. That girl was weak and that girl is dead. I'm a grown woman now. People do grow up, change and move away. I've become an adult, changed and moved on with my life and you should do the same! Tell my mother that you didn't find me!" Lyric said.

"You know what, my job here is done. Your mother hired me to find you and I found you. Now I am leaving. I don't have time for this," Demetrius said.

With an attitude Demetrius walked out of the office.

"Sorry about the beating man," Bull Dog said. "I didn't know you were a friend of Jazzy."

"Don't even worry about it," Demetrius said.

Demetrius walked out of the club and sat down inside the car and drove to his office.

"Well, that didn't go very well," Demetrius said. "This is going to be harder than I thought I guess."

Demetrius spent all night at his office researching more articles on Lyric.

In the meantime at the club, Lyric's heart was filled with pure painful emotions. So she pushed everything off her desk, flipped the desk over, fell on the floor and wept. She had a hangover and chose to sleep all day and night on the floor. The next morning Lyric picked herself up off the floor and went to the bathroom and vomited all the food she ate and the alcohol she drank the last night into the toilet. Then she drove home, took her shower, and drove around the town.

CHAPTER 2

It was midnight and Demetrius heard a knock at the door. The person was knocking as if they were the police and Demetrius was wanted for drug usage.

"It's late, I wonder who is knocking on my office door at this hour," Demetrius said to himself.

The knock became harder and harder. Finally Demetrius got out of his chair and walked to the door.

"Wait one minute, hold on!" Demetrius yelled.

Next Demetrius opened the door. Standing outside soaking wet was Lyric. Demetrius could tell she was weeping because of the black eye liner on her face was running down her cheeks.

"Lyric, what are you doing here?" He asked.

"Demetrius I have come to see you," She said.

"Why have you come to see me?" He asked.

"I don't know," She answered.

"Lyric don't play games with me. Why are you here?" Demetrius asked.

"You know what I don't know why I'm here. I don't know what I'm doing. You know maybe I should just leave," Lyric said.

Suddenly, Ryno and his crew kicked down the door, pulled their guns from their pocket and started shooting massively.

"Sir you're not supposed to be here," Andy said.

Ryan and his boys aimed the gun at her and shot her continually until she fell dead. After shooting her, Ryno and his crew show every person that was visible. A total of 20 people lost their lives.

"Lyric, duck get down!" Demetrius whispered.

They both got down on the floor. Then they both crawled to Demetrius' secret bedroom in the office. Next they got off the floor, ran to the stairway. Then they ran up the stairs as fast as they could. Ryno's boys tried shooting at them and missed. Demetrius pulled the gun from his pocket and shot three of Ryno's boys in the heart and they fell dead. After Demetrius and Lyric reached the highest floor, they found an empty room.

"What are we going to do now?" Lyric said.

"We have to climb out of the window. I know a way to escape," Demetrius said. "Lyric, you have to trust me."

Demetrius grabbed Lyric's hand, and they climbed out of the window. Then they climbed the latter and went on top of the roof.

"He's on the roof get him!" Ryno yelled.

Ryno sent three more of his men to follow them. Demetrius and Lyric ran as fast as they could on the roof. Suddenly they were trapped.

"We have to jump," Demetrius said.

"Are you crazy, we can't jump!" Lyric said

"But Lyric, we must jump, or they are going to kill us," Demetrius said. "I need you to trust me!" He insisted.

Demetrius grabbed Lyric and threw her to the next building. Then Demetrius jumped to the next building. Finally, Demetrius and Lyric ran down a ladder on the side of the building. Then Demetrius pulled the ladder off the building so that the men couldn't come after them. Then they got into Demetrius' car and Demetrius drove away.

"I need to stop at my place," Lyric said.

"We are on the run! I don't think that's such a good idea," Demetrius said.

"Come on, those dudes aren't following us," Lyric said.

"Ok fine, we can do that," Demetrius said.

CHAPTER 3

Demetrius drove to Lyric's apartment. Then he parked the car in the front. They both went into the apartment. Lyric quickly packed a few clothing.

"You have a nice place here," Demetrius said.

"Thank you," Lyric said.

"Ok, we have to hurry up! We don't want the men after us," Demetrius said.

"Look Demetrius! I need for you to tell me what the hell is going on! Why are these psychos after us?" Lyric asked.

"Lyric, we don't have time to explain right now! We need to go now!" Demetrius said.

"Listen, if you don't tell me what the hell is going on I'm not going anywhere with you," Lyric said.

Suddenly, Demetrius looked out of the window and saw Ryno shoot up his car.

"Lyric, we have to get out of here! I just saw Ryno shoot up my car outside," Demetrius said.

Suddenly, Ryno busted the door open. Then Ryno and his boys started shooting and tearing the place up.

"Follow me," Lyric whispered.

Lyric and Demetrius ran to the backyard. While they were getting in the car Ryno left out the house and his boys set the house on fire.

Demetrius and Lyric got into Lyric's Escalade. She sat on the passenger side, and Demetrius sat in the drivers seat. Then Lyric gave Demetrius the keys. Demetrius drove away. Ryno and his boys quickly hopped into the car and followed them. Lyric looked back and saw Ryno following them. Ryno shot at the truck.

"Demetrius, he is on our tail. Demetrius give me your gun! I'll shoot out his tire while you drive," Lyric said.

"Are you sure you know how to use a gun?" Demetrius asked.

"You just have to trust me," Lyric said.

Lyric took the gun and shot out his window and his tire. Demetrius sped up and cut between cars. Ryno's driver bumped into a car. Demetrius and Lyric got away.

"Thank God we lost him," Demetrius said.

"Where are we going now?" She asked.

"Don't worry about it," Demetrius said.

"You know what Demetrius! I am tired of these damn secrets! I'd like for you to tell me where the hell we are going!" She said.

"Woman, I told you not to worry about where we are going! Just sit back, relax, and enjoy the ride! You need to learn to practice your silent voice dang," Demetrius said.

"Whatever," Lyric said.

Lyric had a frown upon her face as folded her arms and rolled her eyes at Demetrius. Then she began to sit there silently! A few minutes later, Demetrius broke the silence.

"Where did you learn to shoot a gun like that at?" Demetrius said.

"Women can shoot guns just as good as men can," Lyric said.

"Seriously, where did you get the skill? I didn't think you would be the type that would pick up a gun," Demetrius said.

"I said it's none of your business. Now stop asking me all those damn questions!" Lyric said with attitude.

"You know what you are an impossible chick!" Demetrius said. "I can't wait to get you back home to your mother. Geesh."

Suddenly there was silence between them. They remain silent for the rest of the ride.

CHAPTER 4

Finally, they arrived at Demetrius' best friend's house. Demetrius got out the truck. Lyric sat in the truck with her hands folded, and legs crossed. Demetrius went back to the truck and opened the door. Then Lyric got out of the truck. They both walked on Antonio's porch. Demetrius knocked on the door.

"Who's there?" Antonio said.

"It's me Michi!" Demetrius said.

Antonio opened the door and let Demetrius and Lyric into the house. Antonio gave Demetrius a hug.

"It's good to see you bro," Antonio said.

"Good to see you too man," Demetrius said. "Antonio, I want you to meet my friend Lyric. Lyric this is my best friend and partner in crime Antonio."

"It's nice to meet you Antonio," Lyric said politely.

"It's nice to meet you too Lyric. I want you to know that I went to see you at the bar a few nights ago. You were awesome," Antonio said.

"Thank you, I'm glad that you enjoyed the show," Lyric said.

"Can you sing us a lullaby or a ballad?" Antonio said.

"Not right now," She replied.

All of a sudden Antonio's baby boy started crying loudly. Antonio's wife Maria came into the living room.

"Honey, this baby just won't stop crying. I fed him, changed him, burped him, but he will not go to sleep. I just don't understand what I am doing wrong," Maria said.

Antonio grabbed the baby and tried to quiet him down, but the baby still screamed and hollered.

"Can I please hold the baby boy?" Lyric asked.

"Yes please do. Let's hope that he respond to you," Antonio said.

Antonio placed the baby boy gently into Lyric's arms. Then Lyric started talking to the baby.

"Honey, why are you screaming? Why are you so fussy? Calm down sweetie," Lyric said. "You know when I was a baby like yourself my mommy used to sing to me when I would cry at night."

Then Lyric sang the song "A New Day Has Come" to the baby boy.

All of a sudden he was quiet. He looked Lyric in her eyes. Antonio and Maria was amazed how their baby boy was so quiet and so receptive to Lyric. Demetrius was impressed. Lyric continued to sing to the baby boy until he fell asleep. Then she followed Maria to the room and gently placed the baby into the baby bed. Lyric pulled out a CD from her bag and gave it to Maria.

"Here is my CD. I want you to have it. That track A New Day Has Come is on it. You can play it when you're trying to get the baby to sleep," Lyric said.

"Thank you so much Madam," Maria said.

"You're welcome," Lyric said.

"Our guest bedroom is not cleaned out, but I am going to clean it out," Antonio said.

"Thank you but that's not necessary because we're not staying here long. We will just sleep in the living room," Demetrius said. "Would it be okay if we stayed here with you for a few days?"

"Of course Michi. You and your girl is always welcome here," Maria said.

"She is not my girlfriend she is just someone I am taking home to her mother," Demetrius said.

"Lyric, you definitely have a way with children. Children must love you," Antonio said.

"Well, I have had 2 miscarriages. I always wanted children, but it never happened," Lyric said.

"I'm sorry to hear that. Please don't cry Lyric," Antonio said.

Maria gave her a hug and comforted her while Antonio went into the bathroom to get Lyric some tissue. Demetrius went outside and grabbed Lyric's clothing and her pictures. Then he went back into the house.

"Lyric, I grabbed some of the photos of you and your family because I wanted to look at them," Demetrius said.

"That's cool," Lyric said. "This picture is a picture of my family which are my mom, brother, myself and Demetrius.

"Wow, what a beautiful family!" Maria said.

"This next picture is a picture of Demetrius' mom, dad, sister, brother, Demetrius and myself. I took a picture with both my family and his family," Lyric said.

"That's a lovely family too," Maria said.

"This next picture that I have is a picture of me and my fiancé Mark. He and I were engaged for about 3 years," Lyric said.

"Fiancé? What do you mean fiancé? Wow, Lyric you didn't tell me you had a fiancé! Where is your fiancé?" Demetrius said.

"Well my fiancé was killed," Lyric replied.

"What happened to him?" Antonio asked.

"It's a long story. What happened is Mark was a thug in a gang and was one of the most dopest drug dealers in town. People around the town were afraid of him even Ryno. Ryno had much respect for him. Mark was powerful. Many people did whatever he asked and when they didn't do what he asked he killed them. So one day Mark left me and went to Chicago. One thing for sure is you can't just think that you're going to run another city just because you're the top dog in the other city. He and his boys stole millions of dollars from this rich white man and killed the man's wife and children. Then the husband was angry because he loved his wife. So he came after me, so I had to spend my life running from him. Then Mark ended up killing him. A new drug dealer moved to Detroit from New York. This guy tried to get me to be with him though he had a wife. I rejected him because I loved Mark. However, he and Mark didn't like each other because Mark was sleeping around with his wife. So to get him back he thought that I was going to sleep with him. I didn't mess around on Mark because

I felt that it's wrong to mess around when you're in a relationship or marriage. Of course, I caught Mark sleeping around, but I stayed with him because I loved him. Mark gave me everything I wanted. He sold the club to Joe and Joe decided that he wanted me to sing there. So that is how I started singing. Mark started getting worst about sleeping around with other people's wives and pregnant women. So I eventually left him alone. At that time, we were staying in an apartment. Mark and Ryno got into a fight because Mark stole billions of dollars from him and killed his children. So Ryno and Slim joined forces (the drug dealer from New York) and they decided that they were going to take Mark out. I overheard them talking and having lunch. So I warned Mark that he has some enemies. I told him everything that was said. Like the childish man he was he went over to Ryno's place and shot at one of Ryno's boys. Some nights Mark came home drunk and beat me. Because I was so stressed out from that man, I had 2 miscarriages. After he hit me for the last time, I moved out. Joe bought me a house because he had a crush on me. Joe also paid all my bills. So one day, Mark was out with his boys and Ryno shot him. Mark was in the hospital for months at a time. I have not heard from Mark, and I don't know if he is dead or alive but I'm hoping he is dead so he can't hurt me or come after me," Lyric said.

"Wow, I tell you that is some crazy stuff," Antonio said.

"Yeah I know. Tell me about it," Maria said.

"I was afraid that Mark might come after me because I left him. I didn't feel safe, so I hired Bull Dog to be my bodyguard," Lyric said.

Demetrius looked deep into Lyric's eyes.

"Lyric, I will protect you. Nothing is going to happen to you," Demetrius said.

"Lyric, who are the two kids in the picture?" Antonio asked.

"Oh that is me and Demetrius when we were little kids. When we were little we used to do everything together. We went to church, to the store together, and shopping together. Every day we used to sit under our favorite tree and read to one another after school. We used to have picnics together, just the two of us. We used to tell jokes to each other. Demetrius had a big head; his head was bigger than his body," Lyric said.

They all laughed.

"I remember those days too. We used to lie together under the tree, resting our head on each other as we enjoyed different novels. Lyric was my best friend back in those days. We had a deep love for one another. I don't know what has happened to her," Demetrius said.

"You left me alone and moved to another state so, I did the same thing to cope with the idea that the man I loved left me. That is what has happened to me," Lyric said.

"It looks like you guys have a lot to talk about. Lyric, Demetrius it was fun talking to you guys. We have to go to bed because we have work in the morning," Maria said.

Everyone said goodnight to each other. Maria and Antonio went to bed.

"Lyric, I didn't know that you felt that way about me," Demetrius said.

"I told you over and over to take me with you! You told me to stay here and, you promised me that your absence would not change our relationship. You also said that you would be back to get me after you were financially stable. But you never did. After high school, you left. I understand that you went to college and moved to Detroit but, you never came back to get me. You stopped calling me. You stopped writing me letters. I went to Detroit to find you but I never found you. My mom always gave me hope she told me that God would bring you and I together. After years of not knowing where you were in Detroit, I stopped believing because you never returned to get me. When I was in Detroit, I was hurting, heartbroken, sad, lonely, and I had no one. I ended up getting raped by 5 different men. I was at work not doing anything to hurt anyone. Trying to be a good Christian woman, I went to church, and did everything I knew to do that was right. I was walking home from work because I didn't have a car. This man got out of his car and asked me if he could take me home. So I said, "No thanks" and kept walking. Then he got out of the car and said, "Baby why can't I take you home?" I just kept walking. Then all of a sudden, he grabbed me. I didn't have any protection. I screamed but no one heard me. He threw me in the car and drove me to this house. He put some duct tape on my mouth. The people at that house were partying and drunk. That man took me upstairs. I was so scared. He said to me, "I am going to do some stuff to you and it won't hurt. If you scream, attempt to escape, or tell anyone about this I will kill you, so I stood there. Then he took off all my clothing, pushed me on the bed and tied me up. Then he stuck his penis inside me. After hours of raping me some of his homies came in and they took turns raping me. I prayed in my mind that God would get me out of that situation. I couldn't move, as I lied in that bed, they all raped me for hours. Then the police walked in and they all left the house. I sat there crying and testified against Slim and his boys because of what they did to me. They went to prison, but that wasn't enough. It still didn't take the pain away. Then I dealt with that man Mark. I thought I would find love through him, but I never did," Lyric said.

Then all of a sudden, more tears ran down Lyric's cheeks. Demetrius wiped away her tears with his hand and hugged her. Then he looked deep into her eyes.

"Lyric, I am sorry that I wasn't your Knight in Shining Armor. I am sorry that I didn't rescue you. I loved you so much, but I wasn't sure how to approach you. I thought maybe you had found someone else. Every day I was here in Detroit I thought about you. I thought about how our life would have been if I had taken you with me. Although, I had been in other relationships, I always thought about you and that is why they didn't last. Hearing about all the pain that you went through makes me feel so sad. I am so sorry that this happened to you. I promise you that I will protect you. I won't let another man violate you. I won't let anything happen to you. I hope that you can forgive me Lyric. I really do love you and I hope that you can forgive me," Demetrius said.

"Demetrius I love you and I always will," She said.

Then all of a sudden, Demetrius put his hands into her pants. She pulled away from him.

"Lyric, I'm so sorry. I didn't mean to touch you. It is just that I love you so much. I didn't mean to disrespect you," Demetrius said.

Then Demetrius tongue kissed Lyric that whole night until she was relaxed.

"Lyric, I won't let another man hurt you again. With all the strength that is in me, I will protect you. I believe that it is destined for us to be together," Demetrius said.

"I won't argue with that. Demetrius I have never loved another man like you before. Just when I was about to give up on men, you came back into my life," Lyric said.

"Well there is a reason for everything that happen it's all in God's perfect will for us to be together," Demetrius said.

CHAPTER 5

Everyone in the house woke up early except for Lyric. Maria and Antonio went to work early that morning and took the children to the baby sitter. After Lyric had woke up, she went into the restroom and took a shower, brushed her teeth, washed her face, put on deodorant and then put on her clothing. Then she sat in the room watching TV.

Finally, Antonio and Maria both got off of work and cooked dinner for them. Lyric washed the dishes and looked after the children after the baby sitter dropped them off at the house.

"Michi, do you love her?" Maria asked.

"Yes I do love her," Demetrius said.

"I think that she loves you too," Maria said.

"Maria, would you go with me to get something right quick?" Demetrius asked.

"Of course Demetrius," Maria said.

Michi drove to Detroit and found the locker that had a lot of money. Maria stayed in the truck. Quickly Demetrius grabbed his duffle bag and put the money in it. Then he drove back to Ohio.

"Maria, I have one more stop ok," Demetrius said.

"Sure," Maria said.

"Don't tell Lyric about this but I want you to help me to pick out something for her," He said.

In the meantime, Ryno and his buddy were looking around in Detroit for Lyric and Demetrius. The first place they looked was at the place where the money was. He figured Demetrius would come there. However, when he busted the locker opened the money was gone. Ryno get very angry, so he called Demetrius. Demetrius answered the phone.

"Hello," He said.

"Demetrius, Demetrius, Demetrius, want to die today don't you?" Ryno said.

"Who is this?" Demetrius asked.

"Demetrius don't act slow! You know who this is. I want my money! I know that you have it. When I find you and your slut both of you are dead and that is a promise," Ryno said.

"First of all, you don't know who you are messing with. I could go to the cops and have you arrested," Demetrius said.

"Demetrius the more I talk to you the dumber you get. I have friends who are cops. There are cops who work for me and I will not go to prison. You're the one who will go to prison for stealing money from me. Try me! It will back fire," Ryno said.

"You know what, forget you. I have a life to live and you better back off," Demetrius said.

"You and your little slut is history when I find you both and that's a promise," Ryno said.

"Leave her out of it! This does not concern her. She has nothing to do with it! Oh and she's not a slut! Don't ever disrespect her like that again or I'll come and kill you myself," Demetrius said.

"You want to save her life then bring me my money," Ryno said.

Demetrius hung up the phone on Ryno. Then Ryno called the number again and Demetrius ignored his call.

"Who is that Demetrius?" Maria asked.

"Maria that was the man that I got in trouble with and his name is Ryno. Lyric and I must leave because I don't want to put you and your family in danger," Demetrius said.

"Demetrius, I am not scared. Our home is not in the newspaper. They won't find you here. Just stay at least one more night and then you can go. You can ask my husband to give you two shotguns. You know he has a lot of them, and he would gladly give them to you for your protection," Maria said.

"Your husband is a lucky man to have an awesome woman like you," Demetrius said.

"Thanks for saying that," Maria said.

"You're welcome," Demetrius said. "Maria, can you talk to Lyric for me. Maybe tell her what you know about me. I don't think she trusts men, and I want her to be comfortable with me. I was her Knight in Shining Armor, and I let her down. This time I want to be there for her. I want to prove to her that I love her. I want to get back into her good grace. Please talk to her."

"I will talk to her," Maria said.

"Thank you so much I really appreciate that," Demetrius said.

"It's no problem Michi. You're a friend of my family so I will do what I can to help you," Maria said.

After Lyric finished washing the dishes she sat to the table. Antonio sat down next to her.

"Lyric, I heard all that you had said last night. I wasn't trying to eavesdrop, but I couldn't help it. I am sorry for all that happened to you. I know who the guy is, if I could get away with it I would go to Detroit and kill him and his boys myself. No man should rape a woman or take advantage of her. I want you to know that if there is anything my wife and I can do for you let us know," Antonio said. "We look at you as family now."

"Thank you," Lyric said.

"You're welcome," Antonio said.

"Now I have a hard time trusting men. The moment a man gets close to me I feel like that horrible night is happening all over again. I don't want to live my life like that," Lyric said.

"If you're referring to Demetrius, I want you to know Demetrius is not like that. Demetrius respect all women. I trust that man with my life. That is why I don't care if my wife drove with him. I don't question his judgment because I trust my wife and I trust Demetrius. That man has been a loyal friend to me for years. As far as other men is concerned, I wouldn't let my wife go anywhere with another man," Antonio said.

"Oh Ok," Lyric said.

"You know something else?" Antonio asked.

"What?" She said out of curiosity.

"Demetrius loves you so much. That man is practically in love with you. No matter what women he dated in the past he always told me that he thought about you. He talked about you so much that I thought maybe you were an imaginary girl because for years, I never saw you. He always told me that he wanted to travel to Georgia and get you," Antonio said.

"I don't understand if he loved me so much why didn't he come to get me?" Lyric asked.

"He saw you on television singing. So he figured that you were in a relationship living somewhere millions of miles away. You know how it is when someone become famous they only want to date famous people. So he decided that he was going to forget about you. The only problem with that was he couldn't. So anyways, one day your mother contacted him because she was afraid for you. She hired him to look for you. I assisted him. Everyone in Detroit knows who you are. My children love to listen to your music. I found a picture of you from the Internet, printed it, and gave it to Him. I found the information that talked about you being in Detroit singing at the club there ran by Joe, so I printed out the information. I saw an article about you in the Detroit Free Press. For years, we had been looking for you. I said all that to say that Demetrius really do love you. Demetrius didn't do this for money, but he did it because your mother asked him to. He told your mom that he didn't want her to pay him. He agreed to do it for free because he loved you enough to put his life on the line to look for you. I told him that taking that case would be too dangerous because Ryno and his crew were after him. But he didn't listen. So I am his friend and I had to support him in all that he decided to do," Antonio said.

"Wow thank you for being a great friend to Demetrius. I am amazed by all this," Lyric said.

"When you love someone you would do all you can to protect that person! I did everything in my power to protect Maria. Maria was with Ryno before she was married to me years ago. Ryno cheated on her and abused her every day. She left him, and I helped her through the pain and moved her away from Detroit. Ryno threatened to kill her if she left him. So I will kill him before I let him find my family. The only reason I haven't killed him yet is because I know my wife and children will need me and I can't go to prison," Antonio said.

"Does Demetrius know all this? I don't think it is a good idea for Demetrius, and I to be here. What if Ryno tracks us down? I don't want to put you and your family in danger," Lyric said.

"Lyric, don't worry about it. Ryno won't find us. No one around this neighborhood knows Ryno. These people are rich white people. They don't know any rich gangsta black people. These people are like my family. If something went down at my house, all of them would come over with their guns. I am not worried. I haven't been in the military for nothing you know," Antonio said.

Finally, Demetrius and Maria arrived at the house.

"Lyric tomorrow morning we are leaving," Demetrius said.

"Ok," She said.

He looked at Lyric. She appeared to be different that day. There was no smart mouth or anything. So Demetrius was trying to figure out what was wrong with her. Maria and her husband were talking to each other in Spanish because they didn't want Lyric or Demetrius to understand what was being said.

"Demetrius, come to the garage with me. I have something important to talk to you about," Antonio said.

Antonio led Demetrius to the garage with him. Antonio gave Demetrius some guns and talked to him about Lyric.

"You know I talked to Lyric today," Antonio said.

"Oh no, man what do you say to her?" Demetrius said.

"Don't worry about it. Just know that her heart is open for you. She is just waiting on you to approach her," Antonio said.

"Lyric, you know Demetrius is really a nice guy," Maria said.

"Ok," Lyric said.

"He talked about you, and I can tell that man love you. The way he looks at you and everything. When you told him about your fiancé, I saw anger rose up out of him. Girl he got it bad for you, you better get him. Before some other woman in this world try to get him. I believe that God intended for the two of you to get married. It is so funny how things happened. Just when he was about to give up on you, your mother called and hired him to find you. That gave him an excuse to find you," Maria said.

"Maria, I do believe that Demetrius is a good guy. But what if I can't love him like he wants me to. I don't know how to love a man," Lyric said.

"Well you know something I didn't know how to love a man. Different men raped me. There was even a time in my life when I went to women. But then after a while, I got tired of that. I was broken but God grabbed me and changed me into the woman that he desired me to be. Then all of a sudden, I stopped liking women. I gave my life to the Lord Jesus Christ and, God sent me my husband Antonio. Antonio was everything that them other men weren't. Open your heart to God, and then open your heart to Demetrius. He is really a good man. He will love, protect, honor, and cherish you at all costs," Maria said.

"I am not ready to be with anyone right now. I guess one day I will get married and settle down and have children. I have to get back out there. The people need me. I am an entertainer," Lyric said.

"Sweetie, that kind of life can get you killed. It's not that God doesn't want you to sing. It's just that God doesn't want you to sing at nightclubs. That is not the plan that God has for you. You will see that God has a plan for your life. His will shall be done in your life," Maria said.

"I lost my faith in God. 5 men raped me. I didn't put myself in that situation either. I still don't understand why that had to happen to me. I had plans on saving myself for marriage. But my innocence and purity was stolen from me. I didn't give it to a man it was taken from me by a man. Do you know how that feels to have your virginity taken from you?" Lyric said with tears in her eyes.

"Yes I know how that feels. I was raped every day of my life when Ryno and I were in a relationship. Then he would let other men have sex with me. Then a few times he threatened to kill me if I didn't have sex with a woman. Though I went through all that pain in my past, I am not going to let my past separate me from God. I am not going to let my past stop me from loving my husband. I will continue to be the best wife I can be to him. And you have to learn to be the same way. I tell you, Ryno did some terrible things to my body. He forced me to have sex with women, all because he enjoyed that kind of stuff. For a long time, I hated him. But I have forgiven Ryno and, I pray that God has mercy on his soul. I am over that. You too have to get over what them men did to you and other men that mistreated you. You will be okay girl. I want you to call me when you're ready to give your life to the Lord," Maria said.

Jason who is one of Maria and Antonio's children walked into the room and sat next to Lyric.

"Are you that singer Jazzy Lady Blue from on television?" Jason said.

"Yes that is me. But don't tell anyone," Lyric said.

"Can I do my report on you? Would it be possible if I took you in my class tomorrow morning for show and tell?" Jason asked.

A few minutes later Demetrius walked into the room.

"Demetrius I want to go to the class and sing for the kids before we leave tomorrow," Lyric said.

"Ok Lyric. We can do that. But we must leave after that and head to Georgia," Demetrius said.

For the rest of the day, Lyric spent time with the children. She helped Jason with his project. She sang songs to the children. The children were her joy. She loved being around them, singing to them and talking to them. That evening she didn't talk to Demetrius, Maria or Antonio, but she stayed in their children's room. They taught her some

Spanish, and she showed them how to sing in French. They loved her so much, and she loved them so much too.

"Lyric still has not come out of the children's room?" Demetrius said.

"No, she has not come out of the room. I can tell that children are her greatest joy. She would make a great mother when she has children," Maria said.

"I can see the love of a mother all over her," Antonio said.

"I know that is true. Our kids don't take to people like they did to Lyric especially our little baby. It was amazing how Lyric was able to sing her to sleep," Maria said.

"Lyric must have a way with children," Demetrius said. "I am learning something new about her every day."

Antonio went to his room and went to sleep leaving Maria and Demetrius to talk.

"So Maria, did you have any luck talking to her?" Demetrius asked.

"Well, I really can't tell. Men have hurt her in her life. So if you want to win her heart then you should just show her love. But the only true way to ease that pain is to turn it over to the Lord Jesus Christ," Maria said.

"I will do all that I can. Thank you for talking to her," He said.

"You're welcome," She said.

In the children's room, Lyric was having a conversation with the children.

"Ms. Lyric when I grow up I want to be like you," Sarah said.

"Honey, you don't want to be like me; I have issues. Just be who you are, and you will be successful. Be good and always obey your mother and father because you only have one," Lyric said.

"Ms. Lyric I have prayed to God that he would allow me the chance to meet you. God answered my prayers; you are here in my house. Thank you Jesus!" Sarah said.

"Well, that's great," Lyric said with a smile.

They all stood up, wrapped their arms around Lyric and gave her a hug.

"Jason, I will be at your school tomorrow to do a small concert for your class. But after that I will be leaving," Lyric said.

"Ok, make sure you be there at 11 a.m.," Jason said.

"I promise that I will," Lyric said.

"Ms. Lyric we don't want you to leave. We love you being here. I'm sure my mom and dad would let you stay here," Sarah said.

"Sweetie, I have to leave. I am going home. I will be back to visit one day if the Lord allows me to. I will miss all of you kids," Lyric said.

"Ms Lyric you can sleep in the room with us," Sarah said.

"I don't want to take up space in your room," Lyric said.

"You can sleep in my bed, and I can sleep next to you. There is room in the bed. It is a full size bed," She said.

"Ok Sarah, I will sleep in here with you," Lyric said.

"So what is it like being a star? Everyone must love you. People probably look up to you," Sarah said.

"Being a star can be complicated. People tend to treat you different. Sometimes I wish that I wasn't a star but a regular person. The media have a field day with your life by putting all of your business in the newspapers and gossip magazines. Cameras always follow you. People come up to you wanting autographs. Well that part is pretty cool, but the rest of it is not all that great. People expect you to be something that you're not," Lyric said.

"If it helps, I see you as a regular person," Sarah said.

Jason walked into the room and took pictures of Lyric and his sister. Then he went to get his mother.

"Mom, can you do a favor for me and take some pictures of me, Lyric, and Sarah?" Jason said.

"Sure," Maria said.

Maria and Jason went into Sarah's room. Maria took a lot of pictures of both her two children and Lyric. Then Sarah took pictures of Lyric and Maria. They went and got the baby and took some pictures of Lyric holding the baby. Maria woke Antonio up to take pictures. Maria took pictures of Demetrius and Lyric. Antonio, Maria, Lyric, the baby, and Demetrius took a picture together. Jason and Lyric took pictures together. Antonio took one picture with Lyric. Lyric took a picture holding the baby. Then they went outside and took a few pictures as a family. Antonio's neighbor held the camera and snapped the picture. They took pictures for the rest of the day. It was 9 pm at night all of a sudden, and then they went into the house. They all went into their bathroom and took a shower. Lyric went into the regular bathroom and sat in the tub for a few hours then she washed her body. Then she put on her pajamas. Then Demetrius took a quick shower. The children went to bed, and Lyric and Demetrius sat on the couch.

"I hope that God one day blesses me with children," Lyric said.

"He will one day," Demetrius said.

"Well, I was invited to stay in the room with Sarah. Good night," Lyric said.

"Good night Lyric," Demetrius said.

Demetrius looked a little disappointed because he was looking forward to cuddling with Lyric. But, at the same time he respected the fact that she loved children and how the children took well to her. Then Lyric went into the room with Sarah. Sarah prayed for Lyric.

"Father God, I come to you in the name of Jesus thanking you for allowing me to pray to you. I thank you God for answering my prayers to meet Lyric. I pray Lord that you bless her everywhere she go. I ask that the bad people don't get her and that you protect her. I ask that you allow her to get home safe and sound. Lord I ask that everything goes well in her life. I pray that you allow me to one day be closer to her. Lord I ask that you bless my mom, dad, and my brother. Lord I ask that you bless me too. In the name of Jesus, I pray. Amen!" Sarah said.

"Amen!" Lyric said.

Lyric sat in the bed writing in her notebook. Sarah went to sleep. Lyric wrote Sarah a letter and wrote her cell phone number on there, and mother's address on the sheet of paper and placed a hundred dollar bill in it. She also wrote Jason a note and placed a hundred dollar bill in it. She also stored Maria's phone number in her cell phone. Then she lied down and went to sleep. Maria and Antonio decided to peek in on their children.

"Wow, I see our kids have gotten really close to Lyric. We may have to take them to see her one-day in concert. Sarah will be crushed when she find out that Lyric is leaving," Maria said.

"They will be alright," Antonio said.

"I sure do hope so," Maria said.

Then they both went back to bed. Demetrius also went to bed.

CHAPTER 6

The next day everyone got up early, took their showers and put on their clothing. Then they drove to the school. However, Lyric and Demetrius went to the store and bought posters of Lyric and CDs to give out to the children.

At the school everyone in the class gave their presentations on people who inspire them. Finally, it was Jason's turn. Jason was disappointed because Lyric wasn't there, but he stood up.

"Well I did my report on the singer known as Jazzy a.k.a. Lady Blue. Her real name is Lyric Blue Perkins. The reason I chose to do my report on her is because she is my favorite singer. I recently met her and she is an awesome woman. She has been through a lot of things in her life, yet through it all she is an overcomer. She went through abuse physically, mentally, emotionally and spiritually. She almost lost all of her faith because of it. But she won 6 Grammy awards, and 6 NAACP awards. She went to college, and she received her Bachelor's Degree in Media Arts and Master's Degree in Drama and Media Studies. She has acted in different plays. She has no children due to miscarriages. I wanted to introduce you all to her, but I can't because she is not here," Jason said.

"You didn't meet the beautiful Lady Blue. You are such a liar. Why would she want to talk to a loser? You met her only in your dreams," One of the classmates said.

The whole class started laughing. Jason had a sad face.

"Class be quiet! Good presentation but where is your show and tell item. I will have to mark your grade down 2 grades if you don't have a visual aid," Mr. Johnson said.

"Sorry I'm late Jason," Sarah said.

All of a sudden, his sister Sarah walked into the classroom.

"Mr. Johnson, hello my name is Sarah. Today I want to introduce Jason's visual aid. She is kind and loving, she has won many Grammy's and NAACP awards. She has been around the world. She speaks French fluently. Her name is Lyric Perkins. She is also known as Jazzy and Lady Blue. Ladies and gentlemen put your hands together for the one and only Jazzy, Lady Blue," Sarah said.

Lyric walked into the classroom.

"I'm sorry I'm late," Lyric said.

She kissed Jason on the cheek and gave him a hug. All the students looked with their eyes widened and their mouth's open. Everyone was surprised to see that Jazzy Lady Blue, a celebrity, was in the classroom for the day.

"Thank you Jason for inviting me," Lady Blue said.

"Hi everyone, if it is ok with your teacher I would like to sing something for you today," Lyric said.

"I have heard so much about Lady Blue in Jason's report, so I want to hear her sing. By the way I'm a big fan," Mr. Johnson said.

"Sarah, Jason, I want you both to pass this out to the class," Lyric said.

Sarah and Jason passed out posters and CDs to all of the students and to the teacher. Demetrius, Maria, Antonio was standing there watching Lyric perform. Maria held the baby. Lyric pulled out her portable microphone. Then she started singing. She sang the songs called "You Were Loved, I'm Alive, If You Ask Me To, and A New Day Has Come". Demetrius recorded her on a camcorder.

Everyone in the room cheered loudly. At that moment, Jason became the most popular boy. People lined up to get autographs from Lyric.

"Jason, your presentation was excellent. So you get an A+ on that part of the presentation. If your paper is real good you will get an A+ on that too. Lady Blue, can I talk to you before you leave?" Mr. Johnson asked.

"I can't stay very long because I have to get back home," Lyric said.

Maria and Antonio both gave Lyric a hug.

"Lyric can I marry you?" Jason asked.

"Boy you are too young for me," Lyric said as she laughed.

"Well, I will be 18 in seven years," Jason said.

Mr. Johnson pulled Lyric in the hallway.

"Madam, you did a wonderful job. It is a pleasure to meet you. Do you think I could have your phone number?" Mr. Johnson said.

Lyric wrote down her phone number for him.

"I am not available to date, but if you ever want me to come back to sing for the children call me," Lyric said.

Then they went back into the classroom. All the children gave her a hug. Sarah and Jason gave her a hug. They all said goodbye to her.

"Ms. Lyric, I am going to miss you. I don't want you to go," Sarah said.

Sarah was sad and had tears of sorrow in her eyes.

"Sarah, I love you sweetie. I will come back to visit you sometimes. I will send you tickets to my concerts, and I will fly here personally to take you shopping. It's a promise ok," Lyric said.

"I love you, you are my best friend Ms. Lyric. I thank the Lord for allowing you to be here with me. You are awesome you are cool. Ms. Lyric I will miss you. Please remember me in all that you do," Sarah sang.

"Wow, this girl has talent. Maybe one day you can sing with me when you're older," Lyric said.

Lyric gave Sarah a hug as she wiped Sarah's tears away. Then Lyric grabbed the baby from Maria's arms and began to speak to him.

"I love you baby boy. I hope to see you when you're all grown up," Lyric said.

Then she hugged the baby.

"Jason, you're a great guy and God will send you the right woman your own age someday," Lyric said.

Then she kissed Jason on the cheek and hugged him. Antonio drove Demetrius and Lyric to the airport. A few hours later, they arrived in Atlanta Georgia. Then they caught a cab to a beautiful five star hotel. The hotel was decorated for couples. Demetrius had the waiter to bring up some Champagne. Demetrius took her to the most expensive restaurant. They ordered their food sat down and ate it. Then they went to their room, turned on the TV and hit Netflix and watched movies. For the rest of that day, they sat in their hotel room. Demetrius and Lyric cuddled together watching the movie called Love and Basket Ball. After the movie went off, Demetrius lit a candle and set there next to Lyric.

"What's on your mind honey?" Demetrius asked.

"Just how perfect this moment is. It feels good being in your arms," Lyric said.

"Lyric, I want you to know that I loved you back in those days, and I still love you today," Demetrius said.

"I love you so much. I'm in love with you and always have been. Now I am ready to love again," Lyric said.

"Lyric you're an amazing woman. I have never met a woman like you," Demetrius said.

"This feels like a fairy tale. I have never been this happy with a man. You are everything he wasn't," Lyric said.

Then all of a sudden Demetrius tongue kissed Lyric passionately. Demetrius put his hand in her shirt. Then he stopped.

"I'm sorry I didn't mean to do that," Demetrius said.

"Why did you stop? Demetrius make love to me. I want to give myself to you. I love you," Lyric said.

Demetrius undressed Lyric and undressed himself. Gently, Demetrius made love to Lyric. Lyric moaned. He made noises too. They loved each other and enjoyed each other in the bedroom.

A few hours later, Lyric and Demetrius both fell asleep after. That morning, Demetrius woke up first and left Lyric sleeping. He had to go and do something. Then he came back. He brought her breakfast in bed.

Lyric and Demetrius spent the whole week just enjoying each other's company. They only made love once because after it happened the Holy Spirit convicted Demetrius about having sex outside of marriage.

"You know, I'm so sorry for having sex with you. Lyric, it's not that I didn't enjoy it. I enjoyed every minute of it. It's just that I always believed that two people should wait until they get married before they have sex," Demetrius said.

"You're right about that. I'm sorry too. My mama raised me to keep my legs closed before marriage too. I just got caught up in the moment. I'm sorry, but you have that sexual effect on me. It's not just sexual, but it's love. I love you very much and always have. Even though I know it's wrong, but you don't know how many times I thought about making love to you under that tree when we were younger," Lyric said.

"I used to have that same thought. But let's just save that until we get married to do the right thing," Demetrius said.

CHAPTER 7

As Demetrius drove down the road, he realized that it was Sunday. A memory brought back to his conscious by God of him and Lyric going to church together. He saw how they praised and worshipped God as little children. So Demetrius drove to the church they used to attend. Both Lyric and Demetrius together walked into the church and sat down. They got there just in time for the message.

"Praise the Lord Saints! I said praise the Lord Saints! Let's all give God the praise and the glory! The Lord is good! The Bible says Oh taste and see that the Lord He is good! Hallelujah!" Pastor Andrew said.

The people got out of their chair and started shouting, praising God, and running around the church.

"His grace is sufficient. I was a fornicator. I slept with many different women back in the days, but God pulled me out of sin. There comes a point in your life when you get tired of sinning against God. I can remember many nights I prayed and asked the Lord Jesus Christ to purge me, to wash me whiter than snow. Sometimes I would feel like I was putting Jesus right back on the cross because I was sinning and doing the thing that God hates over and over again. Yet God had mercy on me. His grace is sufficient. I don't want you all to make the same mistakes I have made. God's Word says flee fornication. For all of you who don't know what fornication is that is when a man and a woman having sexual intercourse with each other and they are not married. When you have sex outside of marriage you not only sin against God, but you also sin against your own body. Ladies and gentlemen God has a plan and a purpose for your lives. God gives grace to the humble. If you've sinned against God, go to God, repent, and he is faithful and just to forgive all your sins and clean you up from unrighteousness. God loved us so much that he sent his son Jesus, and Jesus died on the cross for our sins and on the third day he rose from the dead. Think about this for a minute, we were all supposed to die because the Bible says that the wages of sin is death. However, the Lord Jesus Christ became the thing that he hates so that we can be free. He became sin, which caused God to reject him. He died and rose again. Hallelujah! Glory to God! Thank you Jesus! That is what I call true love. Ephesians 2:8 say that for by grace are ye saved through faith; and that not of yourselves: it is the gift of God. God resist the proud and give grace to the humble. God's grace is sufficient for you, and his strength is made perfect in your weakness and my weakness. It is time to accept the Lord Jesus Christ as your Lord and savior and he will help you to overcome your sins. God's grace is sufficient for you all. Humble yourself says the Lord! The Lord says that you need me! Come on to this altar to receive the gift of the Lord by grace and through faith," Pastor Andrew said. "Is there anyone who wants to give their lives to Jesus?"

Lyric left and went to the bathroom. Then the choir started singing. Then Lyric walked in singing. They sang the song I Surrender All. People looked over at Lyric. One of the church ladies grabbed her by the hand and led her to the pulpit.

"Baby, the Lord wants you to sing this song like you used to," The woman said.

Lyric grabbed the microphone and started singing I Surrender All. The choir started singing as she led them. As she was singing, tears ran down her cheeks, and the Lord touched her in a mighty way. As Lyric began to sing the song people started praising the Lord. Lyric went to the altar and sat in the chair. She had tears in her eyes. Then Demetrius went to the altar and sat next to her. At that moment, both Lyric and Demetrius gave their lives to the Lord. They repeated the sinners' prayer from their hearts and receive the Lord Jesus as their Lord and savior. Then they hugged the pastor and hugged each other. They both had tears in their eyes. After service Lyric and Demetrius talked to some of the people in the church.

"Girl, I saw you on television a few weeks ago," Sister Lynda said.

"Oh ok," Lyric said.

The woman who led Lyric to the altar suddenly disappeared.

"Lyric, it's time for us to go," Demetrius said.

"Ok," Lyric said.

Lyric and Demetrius got into the truck. Demetrius drove over to a house. Demetrius knocked on the door.

"Who is it?" Mrs. Perkins said.

"Mrs. Perkins it's me Detective Demetrius," Demetrius said.

Mrs. Perkins opened the door, and she saw her daughter Lyric. At that moment, she cried tears of joy. She grabbed her daughter, embraced her, kissed her on the cheek and hugged her tightly.

"Lyric, I am so happy to see you. Thank you Demetrius for bringing my baby home," Mrs. Perkins said.

"You're welcome Mrs. Perkins," Demetrius said.

"I am going to cook both of you a big meal," Mrs. Perkins said.

Demetrius stayed there with Lyric for two weeks. Suddenly, he decided that he had to leave.

"I will leave the two of you alone to talk. I have something that I must do," Demetrius said.

"Where are you going?" Lyric asked.

"I will be right back," He said.

"Ok," Lyric said.

Demetrius got into the truck and drove away.

"Momma, I am sorry for all the pain I put you through. It was stupid of me to go to Detroit and leave you. I am hoping that you forgive me for the way I acted towards you," Lyric said.

"Honey, I have already forgiven you," Mrs. Perkins said.

"I love you Mama," Lyric said.

"I love you too baby," Mrs. Perkins said.

Mrs. Perkins fried some chicken, made some homemade macaroni and cheese, jiffy mix corn bread, greens, potato salad, baked beans, and a homemade apple pie.

"Lyric I heard the Spirit of God say that you would die if you didn't return home. God told me all the things that you were going through. He told me that you were raped, you had 2 miscarriages, and you were in an abusive relationship. I prayed for you every night. I had to ask God to have mercy on you and to protect you. Honey, the only way to save you was to hire Demetrius to come and get you. But he wouldn't take the money, bless his heart. I was afraid of losing you. I didn't want to be burying my daughter at a young age. Honey, I have cancer, and I will be dying soon. It could happen any day now. I need you to be strong in the Lord. The Lord will protect you and provide for you," Mrs. Perkins said.

All at once tears of sorrow ran down Lyric's face.

"Mama, you're going to be fine. You're not going to die. You can't die. I love you and I can't lose you. I've already lost 2 people I love; I don't want to lose more. Please mama don't leave me!" Lyric said.

Lyric went in the room and cried for hours. Then the Lord sent his angels to comfort her. She dried her eyes and remembered that she had to be strong for her mom. Demetrius walked into the house.

"I came back Mrs. Perkins," Demetrius said.

"Ok. Demetrius can you please go and comfort Lyric. She is crying. I just told her that I have Cancer and won't live long," Mrs. Perkins said.

Demetrius ran into Lyric's room. Lyric's eyes were red, and she got off the floor.

"Hey honey I told you I would be back. I love you," Demetrius said as he wiped her tears away.

Demetrius held Lyric in his arms and tried his best to cheer her up. Demetrius could smell the aroma of the home cooked meal that Mrs. Perkins was in the kitchen preparing.

"That food smells good. Come on let's go in the kitchen and eat together," Demetrius said.

Mrs. Perkins fixed everyone's plates.

"Heavenly Father, we come together thanking you God for this food for the nourishment for our bodies. We ask that you bless the hands of Mrs. Perkins because she prepared the food. We give you all the glory and the honor in Jesus name we pray, Amen," Demetrius said.

"Amen," Lyric and Mrs. Perkins said.

Then they all started eating. After they finished eating Lyric got up and washed all the dishes. Then she sat back down.

"Lyric, let's go to the bank," Demetrius said.

Demetrius drove them to the bank, but Lyric fell asleep in the truck. Demetrius woke Lyric up, and they all went inside the bank.

"Lyric, I need for you to get me your account information," Demetrius said.

Lyric withdrew some money from her account and then went back into the truck. Then Demetrius took all of his money out of his account and put it into Lyric's account. Mrs. Perkins also put all of her money into Lyric's account.

After leaving the bank, they went to the Bible bookstore. Demetrius bought new Bibles for Lyric and himself. Next they drove to see Demetrius' family.

Demetrius mother was happy to see her son. She invited them to dinner, but they didn't stay. Demetrius gave his mother $1000.

"Who is this Demetrius? Is that your wife? If it is not your wife then you should marry her! She is very pretty," Mrs. Woods said.

"Mom, we are not married yet. This is my best friend and the love of my life Lyric. Remember when Lyric and I always went everywhere together. She is my girlfriend now," Demetrius said.

"She's a good one. I don't know how or why she deal with a big head man like you Demetrius," Mrs. Woods said jokingly.

About 20 minutes later they went back to Mrs. Perkins house. Lyric took a nap for about 3 hours while Demetrius sat under the tree thinking. Then Lyric woke up and saw him outside sitting under the tree. So she brushed her teeth, washed her face, and went outdoors to join him. Like old time Demetrius started reading the Bible to Lyric. Together they studied the Word of God. Demetrius began quoting parts of Proverbs 31 with passion as he looked into Lyric eyes.

"Who can find a virtuous woman? For her price is far above rubies. The heart of her husband doeth safely trusts in her so that he shall have no need of spoil. She will do him good and not evil all the days of her life. She seeketh wool, and flax and worketh willingly with her hands. She is like the merchants' ships; she bringeth her food from afar. She riseth also while it is yet night, and giveth meat to her household, and a portion to her maids. She considereth a field and buyeth it: with the fruit of her hands she planteth a vineyard. She girdeth her loins with strength and strengtheneth her arms. She perceiveth her merchandise is good: her candle goeth not out by night. She layeth her hands to the spindle, and her hands hold the distaff. She stretcheth out her hand to the poor; yea, she reacheth forth her hands to the needy. She is not afraid of the snow for her household: for all her household are clothed with scarlet. She maketh her coverings of tapestry, her clothing is silk and purple. Her husband is known in the gates, when he sitteth among the elders of the land. She maketh fine linen and selleth it; and delivereth girdles unto the merchant. Strength and honor are her clothing, and she shall rejoice in time to come. She openeth her mouth with wisdom, and in her tongue is the law of kindness. She looketh well to the ways of her household and eateth not the bread of idleness. Her children arise up, and call her blessed; her husband also, and he praiseth her. Many daughters have done virtuously, but thou excellest them all. Favor is deceitful, and beauty is vain: but a woman that feareth the LORD she shall be praised. Give her of the fruit of her hands, and let her own works praise her in the gates. I have read to you Proverbs 31:10-31. May the Lord add a blessing to the reader, the hearer and the doer of His Word. Amen," Demetrius said.

"Amen," Lyric said.

"Lyric, I want you to know that every Word that I have read to you from Proverbs describe you. You are that beautiful virtuous woman. I thank God for allowing you to be in my life. Lyric I want you to know that I love you," Demetrius said with a smile on his face, and he touched Lyric's face. "A man that findeth a wife findeth a good thing and obtain the favor of the

Lord. So I am going to pull up the courage to ask you. This is something that I have wanted to ask you since we were little children. Lyric I want to obtain the favor of the Lord. You are a good thing to me, and I want to spend the rest of my life striving to please God and to make you happy. Lyric, I have loved you since we were children. When I left you it hurt my soul, and I could never get over you. Lyric you will make me the happiest man in the world if you would be my wife and take me as your husband," Demetrius said.

Then Lyric had tears of joy running down her cheeks. Demetrius pulled a ring from his pocket.

"Lyric, will you let me make you happy? I will love you far and beyond your pain. You can trust me with your heart. I will be everything that those other men weren't. I want to be the father of your children and your husband. Lyric, will you marry me?" Demetrius said.

"I love you Demetrius and yes I will marry you," Lyric said.

Demetrius placed the ring gently on her finger. Then Demetrius tongue kissed Lyric. After 13 minutes of kissing, Lyric went into the house.

"Mama, oh my God look at this. Mama, I'm getting married. Demetrius proposed to me. Thank you Lord Jesus!" Lyric said.

"Go ahead girl! My baby is finally getting married. Thank you Jesus! Hallelujah!" Mrs. Perkins shouted.

First Mrs. Perkins gave her daughter a hug. Then Lyric and Mrs. Perkins ran around the house shouting, jumping up and down because they were both very excited.

Lyric called Maria and told her the good news.

"Maria, girl guess what?" Lyric said.

"What girl?" Maria said.

"I am getting married!" Lyric said.

"Lyric, you're getting married to who?" Maria said.

"Girl, Demetrius just asked me to marry him," Lyric said

"Oh my God girl, when did that happen?" Maria said.

"He asked me today," Lyric said.

"Wow that is awesome," Maria said.

"Maria, I want you to help me to plan the wedding. I want you to help me to pick out the dress, the ring, the cake and the decorations. I think I want the colors to be pink and purple," Lyric said.

"Wow, those are some cool colors. Whenever you are ready to start getting things together with the wedding let me know," Maria said.

"Next week I want to travel there to pick out my dress. We need to start working on it as soon as possible," Lyric said.

"Ok, let me know when you're ready," Maria said.

"I will girl. So how are the children doing?" Lyric said.

"They are doing fine. Lyric, I want to thank you for having such a positive impact on my children. They love you so much and look up to you. Do you know that ever since you came here my children's grades were really good? I thank you for doing that concert. The whole school was talking about you. They would like for you to sing for the dances they have. But I told them that you are not in town anymore. They wanted me to let them know when you are back in town," Maria said.

"Wow, I never thought that I could have an effect on someone like that. I owe all the praise and glory to Jesus Christ," Lyric said.

"Girl, you got to be kidding! You're a celebrity everywhere! Everybody knows who Jazzy Lady Blue is," Maria said.

"I never knew children liked my music. I always thought only older people liked what I put out there," Lyric said.

"Nonsense girl, you are loved by more than just adults. Children look up to you! All my children talk about is how God blessed them to meet you. Sarah's behavior has changed tremendously. I don't know what you said to my children but whatever you said helped a lot. Thank you for helping my children," Maria said.

"You're welcome," Lyric said.

"If you ever need anything ask me or my husband. We got you! You are family to us," Maria said.

"Thank you I appreciate it. But I have to go and spend some time with my man," Lyric said.

"Oh girl you better not be having sex with that man not until you're married," Maria said.

"Girl, you are too late for that, you should have called and told me that a few days ago. It happened, but we promised God it won't happen again," Lyric said.

"Girl you better keep them legs closed," Maria said.

"I will girl. But these legs will be open all the time after we are married," Lyric said.

"Girl, you're a full bottle of mess," Maria said.

"Ok Maria, I have to go. Talk to you later," Lyric said.

"Ok, bye," Maria said.

They both hanged up the phone. Demetrius sat under the tree by himself. Demetrius sat there praising God and talking to God. After an hour of praising the Lord, he just laid there on the ground under the tree. Lyric went in her room, got her portable DVD player, and came to the tree. With her head laid on Demetrius chest, they both lied on the ground and watched movies. They spent the rest of the evening watching romantic movies such as Love Jones, Jason's Lyric, and many others. Mrs. Perkins came outside with her camcorder recording them secretly and taking pictures of them. Later that evening they went into the house and went to bed; of course they had slept in separate bedrooms.

The next day, Mrs. Perkins had packed all her clothing to go to the Women's Revival. Mrs. Perkins' car wouldn't start so one of the women from church came to pick her up.

Demetrius planned a romantic dinner for two. The two of them wanted to make love but they didn't because they are not married. That day they spend the whole day together. Demetrius took Lyric to see a romantic live play. The cast was excellent. Lyric had tears in her eyes she was so affected by it. Then they went out to eat at a fancy restaurant. After they spent all that time together, they went to the house. They sat there and held one another inside the tree house like they used to do sometimes when they were little children.

"Lyric, I have somewhere that I need to go," Demetrius said.

"Where are you going?" She said.

"I wish that I could tell you but I can't! I don't want you to be upset," Demetrius said.

"Honey you're scaring me," Lyric said.

"Honey, don't you worry I will be back. I promise," Demetrius said.

"I can't have you leaving me again. Demetrius you just always have to mess up the moment," Lyric said with anger in her heart.

"Lyric, what we have is real and, it won't be messed up. But I have a few things I need to take care of," Demetrius said.

"The last time you said that you disappeared for many long years! Haven't I been through enough pain? I lost my father many years ago. I lost my two children! I lost my brother a long time ago! I am losing my mother! I don't want to lose you too. Who will I have if I lose you? Demetrius I love you please don't go," She yelled.

Lyric grabbed Demetrius with all the strength in her body.

"Honey you worry too much. I'll be alright," Demetrius said.

Lyric was hurt deep within her heart, so she cried tears of sorrow.

"I just don't understand. Why you have to leave me?" She said.

"Lyric, I'm not leaving you like the other time. I am coming back. My heart belongs to you. I am coming back for this, and I am coming back for you I promise," Demetrius said.

Demetrius took the necklace that was in his pocket and put it around Lyric's neck. There was a picture of him and Lyric when they were little kids inside the locket attached to the necklace. It was a gift given to him by his grandmother. Then Demetrius tongue kissed Lyric for 10 minutes.

"Honey, I will be back. I promise," Demetrius said.

Then he got into his car and drove away. Lyric stayed at the house worried sick about Demetrius. She couldn't eat or sleep. She stayed at home and cried out to God.

Finally, Demetrius went over to a penthouse in Atlanta. When he got out of the car, a group of men grabbed him, beat him, and tied him to the tree.

"Well, well, well if it isn't Demetrius. I am going to kill you right now," Ryno said.

"Look Ryno, I came to settle this thing with you man to man. I am tired of running from you," Demetrius said.

"Well, now you're about to die. Do you have any last wishes," Ryno said.

"Ryno, your money is in the car. I came to give that to you. I don't want there to be any beef with you anymore. I just want to live the rest of my life in peace without getting chased by you. Ryno man you've won. You got your money now please let me go," Demetrius said.

"Where is the money?" Ryno asked.

"The money is in the truck," He said.

"Ryno, you stay here. If that creep is trying to trick us we will kill him dead," Slim said.

Slim and his boys went to the car and grabbed the money.

"Man you are stupid as hell. You have a lot of balls trying to face me like a man Demetrius. You have won my respect. But you still have to die," Demetrius said.

Finally Slim and his boys came back to into the house.

"I have some business to attend to upstairs. Slim, I want you and the crew to beat the hell out of Demetrius and smoke his ass," Ryno said.

Then Ryno went upstairs to have sex with 8 different women.

Slim and his boys took Demetrius to the bathroom. In the bathroom they beat Demetrius up until he was bleeding. All of a sudden, the police arrived at the house. Slim pulled the trigger and shot Demetrius in the arm. Ryno heard noises downstairs so he put on his clothing and tried to escape but he couldn't because the police had the house surrounded. So he took one of the girls he was sleeping with and went outside and attempt to escape. He held a gun to her head.

"I will kill this broad," Ryno said.

So the men held their fire until they could get a clear shot. Antonio looked all over the house and found Demetrius in the bathtub. Antonio untied Demetrius.

"Man are you crazy? Why didn't you tell me you were coming over here?" Antonio fussed at Demetrius. "Come on, I'm about to get you out of here."

Antonio helped Demetrius sneak through the back door. Antonio grabbed the bag of money and placed it into his car.

"Demetrius, I want you to drive and go home. Save yourself!" Antonio said.

Demetrius listened to Antonio and drove away. Meanwhile, at the house Ryno tripped and the police shot him. Some of Ryno's men killed some of the police officers. The police and Ryno's crew were shooting at each other. Antonio called for back up. Eventually, all of Ryno's crew was dead except for Ryno and Slim. Slim and Ryno was handcuffed, put in the back seat of the police car.

"You have the right to remain silent. Anything you say can and will be used against you in a court of Law. You two will be put away for a very long time. We have been looking for you for many years Slim," Officer Brown said.

Officer Brown got into the police car and drove them to the police station and locked them behind bars. Then they were transferred to the Flint prison system.

Demetrius drove over to Mrs. Perkins house. He struggled to get out of the car. Lyric ran outside to help him.

"Honey, oh my God you're hurt, let me call an ambulance," Lyric said.

Lyric pulled her cell phone from her pocket and called an ambulance. Lyric helped Demetrius sit under their special tree.

"Demetrius, why did you go? I was worried sick about you! Now you are hurt!" Lyric said.

"Lyric my love. I want you to know that I am sorry for all the pain that I have caused you. I am dying Lyric. But before I die I want to know if you love me because I love you so much. I will die a happy man. I will tell God you said hello," Demetrius said.

"No honey, you're not going to die! The police and ambulance will be on their way shortly! I promise I'm going to get you some help," Lyric said.

Lyric ran into the house and looked for the first aid kit but she couldn't find it. She tried to call her mother but her mother didn't respond. She tried to get into the car but the car would not start. So she went to sit back under the tree with Demetrius.

Lyric immediately started crying because her heart was broken.

"I love you Demetrius please don't leave me. You're not dying. The ambulance will be here soon and they will take you to the hospital. You will live. Just hold on baby," She said.

"Lyric, you have made me the happiest man. I want Antonio to take care of you. I am going home," Demetrius said.

"Demetrius please don't leave me! Others have left me! Please God save him! Please God give him life! I love you Demetrius so much," Lyric said.

"Can you do me one favor," Demetrius said.

"What do you want me to do?" Lyric asked.

"I want you to kiss me," Demetrius said.

Lyric gave him a passionate tongue kiss for ten minutes. Next, Antonio pulled up in his car at the house.

"Lyric, how is he doing?" Antonio said.

From the sad look on her face and the tears rolling down her cheeks he could see that Demetrius wasn't doing well.

"Antonio, I want you to take care of Lyric for me. Give the money to Lyric," Demetrius said.

"I will Michi, I promise," Antonio said.

"Man you hang in there. We will get you to the hospital," Antonio said with tears in his eyes.

Lyric and Antonio picked Demetrius up and put him into the car. Then they drove away to the hospital.

"Lyric, I love you," Demetrius said.

"I love you too Demetrius," Lyric said.

Then all of a sudden, there was a bright light that appeared in the car. Suddenly the bright light disappeared and Demetrius died in Lyric's arms. After Demetrius died Lyric's heart suffered with exquisite pain as she cried an ocean of tears with sorrow. Antonio hugged her and comforted her.

"I'm so sorry sweetheart," Antonio said.

"I lost him, I lost another person I loved," Lyric cried and grieved loudly.

She laid her head on his chest not wanting to let him go in the back seat. Finally they arrived at the hospital. The doctors took Demetrius body in the back and he was declared as dead.

A few hours later, Antonio drove Lyric home. When Lyric arrived home she went into her bedroom and cried herself to sleep. She had nightmares so she woke up crying. Antonio was sitting there praying for her. Finally Mrs. Perkins walked into the house.

"Hello Mrs. Perkins," Antonio said.

"Who are you and what are you doing in my house?" Mrs. Perkins asked.

"I am Demetrius friend and partner Detective Antonio," He said.

"Where is my daughter?" Mrs. Perkins asked.

"She is in the room Mrs. Perkins," Antonio said.

Mrs. Perkins went into the bedroom to see Lyric. She found Lyric crying and laying on the bed.

"What is wrong my dear?" Mrs. Perkins asked.

"God took him away Mama it hurts. God took the man I love away Mama. God took Demetrius away Mama. I told him not to go but he wouldn't listen to me," Lyric said with tears of sorrow in her eyes.

Mrs. Perkins grabbed her daughter and cried with her. She comforted her daughter and held her close.

"I am so sorry dear. You're going to be okay. I'm here for you baby," Mrs. Perkins said.

Mrs. Perkins held her close to her and prayed for her silently in her Spirit. Antonio went into the car and pulled out the moneybag.

"Lyric, this is the money from Demetrius account. He wants you to have this," Antonio said.

Mrs. Perkins took the money and sat it in Lyric's cabinet. That evening Lyric took a shower and got out of her clothing that was filled with blood and put on some clean clothing. Then she came out. She sat there depressed and very hurt in her heart.

"Lyric, if you ever need anything call me. I will stay here with you for a couple of weeks but then I will go home," Antonio said.

Antonio took care of all of the funeral arrangements for Lyric and informed Mrs. Woods that her son Demetrius had passed away.

CHAPTER 8

That evening Lyric went to sleep and had many nightmares about her twins' death and Demetrius death. So she woke up crying to God. When Mrs. Perkins heard her crying she woke up to check on her and comforted her. Later that day, Lyric read her Bible, and she prayed to God.

"God please give me strength to let go and move on," Lyric said.

She had the strength to go and look for a job. Antonio stayed in the guest room. He tried to support Lyric in every way because He promised Demetrius that he would take care of her. Antonio called his wife on the phone.

"Hey honey," Antonio said.

"Hey sweetheart, where are you? Where have you been?" Maria asked.

"I'm sorry I forgot to call you, but Demetrius was killed," Antonio said.

"Oh no, I'm sorry to hear that honey. Where is Lyric? How is she doing?" Maria said.

"Lyric is having a hard time dealing with it. Please keep her in your prayers. That woman loved Demetrius just as much as you love me," Demetrius said.

"I know. She had called me yesterday and told me that she loved him and that they were getting married. She wanted me to help plan the wedding," Maria said.

"Honey, I know this is a lot to ask of you, but you do trust me right?" He asked.

"Of course sweetheart," Maria said.

"Honey, I promised Demetrius that I would take care of Lyric before he died. I want to stay here for a couple of months with her until she get through these things," Antonio said.

"You could just bring Lyric here. The kids would love it," Maria said.

"Right now Lyric is here taking care of her mother. So she can't just leave her mother," Antonio said.

"Ok then sure you can stay down there honey. I trust you and I trust Lyric," Maria said.

"Ok honey. Thanks for understanding. I love you," Antonio said.

"I love you too," Maria said. "I'll talk to you later honey."

"Talk to you later baby bye," Antonio said.

They both hanged up the phone. Then he walked into Lyric's room.

"Lyric, I just came in here to check on you," Antonio said.

"I am hurting still in my heart, but I know that God will help me to get through this," Lyric said.

"I will be there for you," Antonio said.

"I appreciate that but go home to your wife. You have a wife and children at home. You can't just desert them," Lyric said.

"Lyric don't worry about it. I know that I have a wife and children at home. I talked to my wife, and she is okay with me staying here with you to help you out for a while. Plus I promised Demetrius that I would look after you. Now I will stay here for two months then I will leave. My wife has plenty of money in the bank to cover the bills, and if she needs more I can send more. Don't you worry; I will help you through this. I want you to know that you can leave this place if you want and come and stay with my wife and I. I'm sure that my kids would be happy with that decision as well," Antonio said.

All of a sudden there was a knock on the door.

"Is Miss Lyric Perkins there," The delivery guy said.

"It is I," She said.

"I have a package here for delivery," He said.

"Thank you sir," Lyric said.

"You're welcome beautiful lady," He said.

"You're welcome," She said.

Then Lyric signed for the package. Lyric also went into the mailbox and got the other mail out. In the box were some of the Demetrius things. Lyric opened a letter and started reading it.

"Dear Lyric, my love. I know you probably won't get this letter until tomorrow, but I have some things to share with you.

I want you to know that I love you more than anything. I left you because I was in trouble and didn't want to involve you in it. But you are the first and the last woman that I have ever loved. I am so in love with you. I did everything I could to protect you. That's what a man does when he loves a woman. You are the only one I was in love with. I was in a lot of trouble and made the wrong decisions in my life. I didn't want you to suffer for the mistakes that I made. Ryno wanted to kill me, and I didn't want him coming after you, so I went to him. Honey, I had every intention on marrying you. More than anything I wanted to make you happy. I was willing to do anything to make sure you were safe even if it meant risking things and getting my life taken from me. Lyric, you made me the happiest man in the world when you said yes. I was looking forward to making you my wife. In this box are the keys to my business, the keys to my house in Detroit, and everything else. Those are also my ID and everything. Soon you will get a card in the mail to my account because I put you on there. Every piece of information that I have left is in this box. I even put you on my life insurance policy. Lyric, please don't cry. I want you to get over me. God will send you a man that is much better than me. I didn't deserve you in the first place. Maybe one day we will meet again in Heaven. Continue to draw strength from the Lord Jesus Christ. I love you and always will. Also, tell Antonio to please take good care of you for me. Love, Demetrius," Lyric read as tears ran from her cheeks. Then she sat the box on her floor. Antonio read the letter.

"Lyric don't cry. Demetrius would want you to be strong, and move on," Antonio said.

"I know, but it's just so hard. I need the strength from the Lord to move on," Lyric said.

"Just ask the Lord for joy because the joy of the Lord is our strength. Troubles don't last always! Weeping may endure for a night, but joy will come in the morning. God is your present help in times of trouble. You're going to get through this," Antonio said.

Every single day for two months Antonio stayed there and took care of Lyric. He took her everywhere she needed to go until she bought herself a new car. He helped her to take care of her mother. Then after the two months he went back home to his wife. He felt like Lyric was making progress, so he went back home. Lyric received the money from Demetrius insurance policy and placed it into her account. She also received her card that went to Demetrius account.

CHAPTER 9

After Demetrius had died, Lyric and her mother Mrs. Perkins developed their mother and daughter relationship. They went to the movies, out to eat, amusement parks, beaches, vacations and many other places. Lyric even took her mother with her on tour when she would sing in different places.

"I have good news for you Jazzy," Joe said. "Your album is number one on the chart. I want to give you your check."

Lyric opened the mail and saw a check for 500 million dollars.

"Mama, look! Hallelujah! Thank you Jesus!" Lyric said with excitement. "Mom, let's go celebrate!"

"Yes the Lord is good indeed dear! Hallelujah! Glory to God!" Mrs. Perkins said as she started jumping up and down.

Mrs. Perkins and Lyric hugged each other and rejoiced all day long. Next Lyric made reservations at a restaurant for her and her mom.

"Lyric, I have a few things that I want to say to you. I know that I haven't told you this enough when you were younger but I love you. I also want you to know that I am very proud of the woman you have become. I am so proud of everything you have accomplished so far. I want you to forgive me for not supporting you when you were younger. I also want you to know that I have enjoyed all of your shows especially the ones I was present at. You have a beautiful gift and I want you to keep using it for the Lord and God will continue to prosper you," Mrs. Perkins said.

Tears of joy ran down Lyric's cheeks. The kind words her mother spoke touched her heart in a special way. That was the first time in years that she heard her mother speak positive words to her.

"Mom, I love you too very much and it feels good to know that you are proud of me," Lyric said.

Mrs. Perkins looked at her daughter and suddenly her body clasped to the floor.

"Mama, Mama, Mama are you okay?" Lyric said. "Please Mama, speak to me!"

Mrs. Perkins was unconscious and did not respond to Lyric. Lyric called the Ambulance. The ambulance came and took Mrs. Perkin's body to the hospital. Lyric drove to the hospital. Lyric and waited for hours in the lobby area.

"Miss, I'm sorry to report to you that your mother didn't make it," Doctor Jones said.

After hearing the news Lyric fainted. Then the doctors took her to a room to give her medical attention.

Lyric spent a lot of time with her mother until her mother died. The day when Lyric woke up and found out that her mother was dead, tears of sorrow ran down her cheeks. A deep depression fell upon her. Lyric sat at the hospital crying because her soul was deeply hurting. First she lost her two children due to a miscarriage. Then she lost the man that she was in love with and now she has just lost her mother. After leaving the hospital, she spent time in her room and cried for long hours.

At the church, they had the home going service for Mrs. Perkins. Some people were sad, but others were rejoicing. Lyric sat there and cried. She felt alone. She tried to keep a smile on her face even though inside she was hurting. She consulted God every day and studied the Bible every day. Her mother would have wanted her to get closer to God. She started relying on God for courage, strength, love and comfort. She was hurting inside from all the deaths in her family. However, she couldn't live in that house anymore. She put a for sale sign up and cleaned the house real good and got everything fixed. Lyric packed all her clothing. She paid moving people to move her things to Detroit. A gentleman bought the house for $90,000 cash. So she placed all the money she had in the bank. Then she drove to Detroit. She also moved into Demetrius' big house. She decided to call Maria.

"Hello," Maria said.

"Maria, my mom died," Lyric said.

"I'm sorry to hear that honey," Maria said.

"Maria, I don't want to be alone," Lyric said.

"Are you still in Georgia?" Maria asked.

"No, I'm in Detroit at Demetrius' house," Lyric said.

"I can come and get you when my husband gets off of work," Maria said.

"OK," Lyric said.

Five hours later Antonio got off of work.

"Honey, Lyric is sad and lonely. I want to go and get her," Maria said.

"She said that she didn't want to come here," Antonio said.

"But honey her mother died. She sold everything and moved to Detroit in Demetrius' old house," Maria said.

"Honey, I will go get her because I know where Demetrius lived," Antonio said.

"But I told her that I would come and get her. So let me go. I know where Demetrius lived," Maria said.

"OK then, I will let you go and get her," Antonio said.

Maria drove to Detroit over to Demetrius' house. Maria saw her and gave her a hug.

"Maria, I'm glad you're here. I need a friend right now. Please pray for me," Lyric said as she gave Maria a hug.

"I'm so glad that you are here. Since you have been through so much I want you to stay in my house. I'm not taking no for an answer this time," Maria said.

Maria and Lyric got into the car and drove to the house. It took them an hour to get there. Antonio cleaned up the guestroom so that Lyric could sleep in there. Lyric was sad about losing her mother but she took comfort in the fact that she was about to see Maria's children because she had a deep love for them.

Finally, they arrived at the house. It was summer vacation for the kids, and they were at camp. Maria and Lyric went into the house.

"Oh, I'm so tired. I need to lie down. I have had too much movement today," Lyric said as she looked around for the bed.

"Lyric are you sure you're okay?" Maria asked.

"I'm fine really," Lyric said.

"Ok." Maria looked at her strangely.

Antonio walked into the living room.

"Hey Lyric. How are you doing?" Antonio asked.

"I'm doing fine." Lyric said.

He gave her a friendly hug.

"I am tired can I please go to bed?" Lyric said.

"Sure if that's what you want," Antonio said.

Lyric slept for 3 days straight. Maria and Antonio were trying to figure out what was wrong with Lyric. She was sleeping a lot. And when she woke up she ate about 3 plates of food and was hungry again.

"Honey, there is something different about Lyric," Antonio said.

"Yeah, she depressed! She has lost her babies, she lost the man she loved and she just lost her mother," Maria asked.

"I pray that God heals her heart," Antonio said.

Lyric walked into the living room with them.

"Lyric honey, are you okay?" Maria asked.

"Of course I am okay," Lyric responded.

"Good, I was just making sure because you have been sleeping for days," Maria said.

"Oh I'm sorry I forgot to tell you guys," Lyric said.

"What is going on girl?" Maria said.

"I am 2 months pregnant with twins," Lyric said.

"So that explains why you were eating so much," Maria said.

"Yes, Demetrius would be so happy if he were here. They are his children," Lyric said with a smile on her face.

"Oh ok. We will do what we can to make you feel comfortable here," Maria said.

Finally, Maria and Antonio's children came into the house. They saw Lyric and hugged her.

"Sarah, Jason don't be rough in hugging her. She's got two children in her stomach," Antonio said.

"Can we throw the baby a baby shower?" Sarah said.

"Of course. If that's alright with you Lyric," Maria said.

"Yes, that's fine with me," Lyric said.

CHAPTER 10

All of Lyric friends and Maria friends were sitting in the music hall. The place was decorated in Lyric's favorite colors, pink and purple. Lyric and Karen were in there separate homes getting dressed. Then Marie drove Lyric and Demetria to Maria's house.

"Wow, you ladies look great especially my beautiful wife Maria, and my daughter Sarah," Antonio said.

"Thank you honey, you look handsome yourself. But don't forget about our sons Jason and Joshua," Maria said.

"Yeah you both look good together," Lyric said.

"Thanks Lyric, you're gorgeous and so are your daughters. As a matter of fact we all look good," Maria said.

"Oh yes," Jason said.

"Lyric, Maria we all have a surprise for you," Antonio said.

"What's that," Maria said.

"We're not going to tell you mom," Sarah said.

"It's my concert you guys. I'll be performing," Lyric said.

Antonio tied a scarf on Maria's eyes. Marie tied a scarf around Lyric's eyes.

The limo driver pulled up at the door and opened the door for Lyric and Maria to get in. Then Demetria, Marie, Sarah, Joshua, Jason, and Antonio all got into the limo with her. When they arrived at the Music Hall the crowd was cheering wildly, and paparazzi were taking lots of pictures. Fans were asking for Lyric's autograph. Lyric wasn't able to give an autograph because her eyes were covered. Lyric, Maria, Demetria, Marie, Sarah, Joshua, Jason, and Antonio were escorted into the building by the security guards. After all of Lyric, Maria, and their special guests arrived Lyric's fans were allowed to participate in the celebration to fill up the seats. The place was packed. Joe and Bull Dog were sitting with the celebrities because they were also on the list of people to invite. Mrs. Wood also sat with them. Demetria went on stage and took the microphone.

"Hello everyone. I need you all to quiet down so you can hear me. I am Demetria, Lyric's daughter. Today is my mother's birthday and her friend Maria's birthday. My mom thinks that you all are just here to hear her sing. But what she doesn't know is that she has some special guests in the house and that we're celebrating her birthday. Now this is what I want you guys to do. When my mother and Maria comes on stage I want all of you to sing happy birthday as loud as you can to them," Demetria said.

Backstage, Antonio untied the scarf off of Maria's eyes and off of Lyric's eyes. Then Antonio escorted Maria and Lyric to the stage and the crowd started singing happy birthday to Lyric and Maria. Both Lyric and Maria were very surprise to see all the people. Mr. Johnson and Antonio came out with a cake for both Lyric and Maria. Tears of joy ran down Lyric and Maria's face.

"Mama, we just want to say happy birthday to you and Maria. We love you and may God bless you. We want to thank you both for raising us to be the woman we are today," Marie said.

"You both have always been my hero," Sarah said.

Then they left the stage and sat in the front row.

Antonio and Mr. Johnson sat the cakes on the table and then they got off stage. Lyric and Maria walked over to the cakes, blew out the candles and then walked back to the stage. Maria picked up the microphone.

"I want to say thank you to my family, my wonderful husband Antonio, my beautiful children Sarah, Joshua, and Jason. I love each of you, and I'm grateful that you would do something so wonderful for Lyric and I. I also want to say thank you to my Godchildren Demetria and Marie. I am blessed and feel honored that God and Lyric would allow me to be a part of your lives. I want to thank you both for allowing my family to be a part of this special moment. I want to thank Lyric. Even though I know Lyric didn't plan this, but I do know that she would have planned this if you guys didn't. Demetria, Marie you guys have your mother's heart and God's Spirit, and I truly thank God for you both. Last but not least, I want to say thank you to my Lord and savior Jesus Christ because I know without him none of this would even be possible. Thank all of you for coming. God bless," Maria said.

Next Maria looked over at Lyric and handed her the microphone.

"This is your moment," Maria said.

Then Maria walked off of the stage.

"Hello everyone! I really wasn't expecting this at all. I want to say my special thank you to the people who mean the most to me. First, I want to say thank you and give, honor, praise and worship to my Lord and savior, Jesus Christ. I know without him I would not even exist. I love God my Lord and savior Jesus Christ more than anything or anyone. Second, I want to say thank you to a woman who is very dear to my heart. My mother. When I was going through all of my pain of losing my children due to miscarriages, my mother was praying for me even though she was far away. When I reconnected with her, she was there for me when I lost the love of my life. So tonight, I want to give honor where honor is due. I thank God for my mother, Mrs. Marie Perkins. Rest in peace mama. Third, I want to give honor to the man that God placed in my heart Demetrius Woods. God used him to protect me when I was living in a state of darkness. God used him to lead me back to Christ. He is the love of my life and the father of my children. Rest in peace, Demetrius Woods. I give honor to Mrs. Woods for raising such a great son. I also want to give honor to my best friends Maria and Antonio for being there for me when I lost Demetrius and my mother. Those two had my back, invited me to live in their home. When I went on tour, they took care of my beautiful daughters. Thank you so much. I love you guys, and you're the kindest spirits I know. I also want to say thank you to my beautiful twin girls Demetria and Marie and to my beautiful Godchildren Sarah, Jason, and Joshua. You kids are amazing. I'm so proud of you all, and I want you all to know that I love you. You guys are such a blessing. Thank you for putting this whole event together. I feel honored that you would do all this for me. I also want to say thank you to Joe for giving me the opportunity to sing at his club. I want to thank Bull Dog for always protecting me. I also want to thank all of my fans for supporting me. All of you who are here mean a lot to me. I love you all," Lyric said.

Next the crowd cheered wildly. Lyric looked around and saw all of her celebrity friends were in the audience. She invited Tamela Mann to come up and sing Take me to the King and Safety in His Arms. She invited Smokie Norful to come up and sing I Need You Now and God is Able. She invited Donnie McClurkin to come up to sing Stand. She invited Hillsong to come up and sing Mighty To Save & There is None Like You. She invited Marvin Sapp to sing My Testimony and Never Would Have Made It. She invited Cece Winans to come up and sing I Surrender All and Alabaster Box. She also invited other artists to perform too. After the artists performed, they all sat down in their seats.

"Celine Dion, could you please come to the stage," Lyric said.

Celine Dion walked on the stage.

"Can you please help me by singing I'm Alive with me," Lyric said.

Celine started singing the song I'm Alive and Lyric jumped in to sing it with her. The crowd was constantly cheering. Then Celine Dion singed A New Day Has Come. Next she singed Because You Loved Me. Then Celine Dion took her seat.

"There is one more artist who I wish was here. I wish Whitney Houston were still here. I want to do a special contribute to Whitney Houston. She along with Celine Dion has always been my favorite pop artist. I love the song Count on Me. Cece as a special contribute to Whitney Houston can you please sing that with me," Lyric said.

Cece Winans went to the stage and grabbed a microphone, and they began to sing the song together. The crowd cheered even more. After they finished singing together Cece Winans hugged Lyric and took her seat.

"Now, I am going to do a special contribution to Whitney Houston by myself. This is dedicated to Whitney Houston and to all the people in my life who loved me. I don't even have to name any names you already know who you are," Lyric said.

The crowd continued to cheer loudly. Lyric singed the song You Were Loved. Then she singed the song I have Nothing. Then she singed the song, I Wanna Run To You.

"Everyone, I am going to sing two more songs. These two songs are very special to me. The first song is My Heart Will Go On. The reason this song is special to me is because every time I hear Celine Dion sing this song I think about the great memories I had with Demetrius. I have dreams about him every night," Lyric said.

Next Lyric started singing the song and tears of sorrow ran down her face. Everyone in the audience could feel her emotions, and they began to cry too. After she finished singing that song, she started singing the song I Will Always Love You. The crowd was crying with her as she singed the song.

"I'm done singing now. I just want to say to my mama who is in Heaven, if you're listening and watching over me that I'll always love you. I also want to say to Demetrius, my one true love who is also in Heaven chilling with Jesus that I will always love you. I want to say to my two children who are in Heaven that I will always love you. I want to say to my other children Demetria and Marie, my friends, Maria, Antonio, my

Godchildren, Jason, Sarah, and Joshua that I will always love you. I want to say to my fans that I will always love you. I want to say to my friends, and all the artists who took time out of their busy schedules to support me, I will always love you. I want to say to God, the Lord Jesus Christ, and the Holy Spirit that I will always love you. Thank you all for coming. God bless you all," Lyric said.

All of the artists walked on the stage and began to give Lyric a hug one by one. The crowd became silent and was wiping their eyes. A few hours later, Lyric left the stage and went to the back room. The security guards escorted all the fans from the Music Hall. Then Lyric, her family and friends left, went to dinner at a private restaurant and ate food, cake and ice cream. Lyric didn't eat because she didn't feel like eating anything.

"Mom that man over there is looking at you. I think you should go and talk to him," Demetria said.

"No thanks," Lyric said.

"Why not?" Maria said.

"I'm still in love with Demetrius. I know he's gone, but I still love him," Lyric said.

"I'm sure he would want you to go and talk to that man who has been eyeballing you ever since the concert first started," Maria said.

"Yeah, go talk to the man," Antonio said.

"No," Lyric said. "I would feel guilty to get with someone else. I would feel like I am cheating on Demetrius."

Mr. Johnson walked over to the table where Lyric was sitting.

"Hi Madam my name is Joseph Johnson. I just wanted to come over here to say that you singed beautifully tonight. I've always been a fan of yours even when you were working at Joe's Music Club. Happy Birthday Lady! I was wondering if you would allow me to take you out?" Mr. Johnson said.

"Mama, the man just asked you out! Go ahead and say yes!" Demetria said.

Lyric looked at him and smiled. Then she looked at Mrs. Woods.

"Lyric, it's okay for you to go out and have a good time with someone else. My son is gone. He would want you to meet a nice guy, fall in love again and live a happy life," Mrs. Woods said.

Lyric took a moment and thought about it and then she came to a decision.

"Yes, sure I'll go out with you," Lyric said.

"Can you come out with me tonight?" Joseph said.

"Well, I'm kind of here celebrating my birthday with my family. I don't want to be rude," Lyric said.

"Girl, go ahead! We will be fine! The girls can go home with me," Maria said.

"Yeah mom we'll be fine. Go ahead and go out with that man!" Marie said.

"Mom, it's your night! Go ahead and have a great time! We will be alright," Demetria said.

Lyric looked at Joseph. Joseph reached out his hands and pulled her out of the chair.

"Sure, I'll be happy to spend the rest of this evening with you," Lyric said.

Joseph grabbed Lyric by the hand and they walked out of the building. He opened the car door for Lyric to get into the car. Then she got in the car, and he closed the door. Next he got into the car, closed the door, and drove Lyric to another restaurant. The restaurant was reserved just for the two of them. The only person that was there was the chef and the music DJ. The room was decorated romantically. Rose petals were spread all over the floor in a heart shaped and on the tables. Two candles were lit, and two champagne glasses, along with silverware and plates were sitting on the table across from each other on top of the beautiful white tablecloth.

"This is beautiful," Lyric said.

"This is all for you a beautiful Princess," Joseph said.

"Thank you very much," Lyric said.

"You're welcome," Joseph said.

"Where is everyone?" Lyric said.

"I reserved this spot just for you and me," Joseph said. "Will you dance with me?"

"Yes of course," Lyric said.

The song called When I Fall In Love was playing, and Joseph held Lyric in his arms and they danced the night away.

About The Author

Movie Geek publishes different types of books that was inspired by movies or could be a movie one day. Movie Geek will be publishing fiction and nonfiction books. Movie Geek will also be publishing Romance, Suspenseful, Horror Novels and many other genres. Movie Geek is a big fan of different types of movies and will do reviews on different movies.

OTHER BOOKS BY MOVIE GEEK

Movie Geek plans to write and publish the following titles:

Evil Hell Master

Kelly

The Crazy Man

The Magic Girl

Movie Geek also plans to write and publish many other titles as well. So please do look for other titles in the future.

ONE LAST THING...

If you enjoyed this book or found it useful I'd be very grateful if you'd post a short review on Amazon. Your support really does make a difference and I read all the reviews personally so I can get your feedback and make this book even better.

If you'd like to leave a review then all you need to do is type the link in your browser:

The review link on this book's page on Amazon here: https://www.amazon.com/review/create-review?ie=UTF8&asin=B00HG5BSK8&channel=detail-glance&nodeID=&ref_=dp_top_cm_cr_acr_wr_link

Thanks again for your support!